Fish Guts And Other Bedtime Stories

By

Jamie Bryant

ISBN: 1-4033-6747-7 (e-book)
ISBN: 1-4033-6748-5 (Paperback)
ISBN: 1-4033-6749-3 (Dustjacket)

Library of Congress Control Number: 2002095144

This book is printed on acid free paper.

Printed in the United States of America
Bloomington, IN

1stBooks - rev. 01/16/03

ACKNOWLEDGMENTS

I am forever indebted to Mindy von Atzigen, who I consider a sweet friend for her gift of time she gave in editing this book. If she had only edited the pages, I would have been forever grateful. However, she did more than that. She saw who I really was as a young girl and read history between the lines I had written.

For all the children in the classes I substituted, thank you for being an awesome audience. Your attentive eyes inspired me to write on.

A special thanks is due my husband, Dennis, who encouraged me to pursue my dream of writing. I love you. I'd like to tell my three children, Jared, Boaz, and Cherith that there is no need to roll your eyes anymore when I offer to read you one of my stories because I have a new audience. The sky is the limit, so follow your dreams.

The title of this book

is dedicated to my

dear cousin,

Annette.

I know we

will both

forever

remember that

summer afternoon

in my front yard.

DEAR READER

Forgiveness was the beginning inspiration for this book. With forgiving comes forgetting. If we have truly forgiven someone who has wronged us, we will try with everything from within to also forget. I have some unpleasant memories from my growing up years, and as I got older I found myself dwelling on those memories. Because of my unforgiving heart, I had let the good memories vanish and chose only to remember the bad. This only fed the resentment I was harboring.

True forgiveness came when I took a pen and paper and began this book. Writing stories from my childhood about the happy, adventurous, and fun things we experienced as a family opened my heart to remember the good times.

I would now like to share those with you. Be blessed!

CONTENTS

THE SPANKING

I will always remember my first grade teacher. Her name was Mrs. Ball. Mrs. Ball was of medium height and had brownish gray hair, which she wore in a perm style. She wore glasses, was very thin, and had freckles on her face and arms. There may have been freckles on her legs too, but she wore old, drab, homely dresses down to her ankles and brown, baggy hose, so no one really knew.

I suppose she was a good teacher because I learned the basics and made it to the second grade. However, she was not like my kind, sweet grandma who had babysat me since I was three months old. Mrs. Ball didn't smile very much, and I'm not even sure she liked children. At any rate, she was my first grade teacher.

This particular day seemed routine. Mrs. Ball taught that morning, using the chalkboard for examples. We went to lunch at twelve thirty and afterwards returned to the classroom. Part of our after-lunch routine was to place our heads down on our desk and rest for thirty minutes to an hour. I suppose this was to digest our food or maybe to get us really sleepy so we wouldn't cut up during the afternoon lessons. This day was no different, and after giving the word to place our heads down on our desks, Mrs. Ball turned out the lights.

Then Mrs. Ball did something she had never done before. She quietly announced to the class that she was stepping out for a minute and we were to keep our heads down and no one was to get up out of their seats for any reason. She had only been gone for a couple of minutes when Jimmy, one of the class clowns, got out of his seat and walked to the blackboard. He grabbed the only eraser our classroom had and tossed it across the room under Angela's desk. Angela wasn't about to get in trouble when Mrs. Ball came back in, so she subtly leaned over, picked up the eraser and tossed it across the room under another student's desk. This quiet tossing of the chalkboard eraser continued for what seemed like hours, but was actually only a few short minutes. Well, you've probably already guessed by now that the eraser eventually landed under my desk.

I looked around trying to figure out who exactly threw it. After a glance or two around the room, I realized it didn't really matter who threw it. I just needed to get rid of it. Should I throw it under someone else's desk or should I take this as an opportunity to put the eraser back where it belonged? Time was running out, and I had to act quickly. You could have heard a pin drop in that classroom as I reached under my desk and scooped up the eraser. "I must be quick," I thought to myself as I hurried to the chalkboard and placed the eraser back in its place. As I turned around, we all heard the sound and looked up in unison as the door opened and in walked Mrs. Ball. The look on my face must have shown shock or guilt because her question was directed totally to me.

"Jamie, why are you out of your seat?" she said sternly.

As I opened my mouth to answer, Mrs. Ball interrupted my words with, "It really doesn't matter. You heard the rules when I left the classroom."

In her cold voice she said, "Come here!"

I slowly walked over to her desk. She took her large, brown, wooden chair, brought it around to the front of her desk, and firmly sat down.

"Bend over my lap here and receive your punishment," she commanded.

A hundred thoughts went swirling through my head all at once. "I'm innocent!" I thought to myself, but this wasn't changing my situation. Then, all at once, I looked down and realized I was wearing a dress and boots.

"Jamie Horton, did you not hear me?" Mrs. Ball exclaimed.

I nodded and proceeded to slowly walk toward her with pleading eyes. I made one last attempt to look to my classmates to see if anyone was going to speak up for me. We were all six years old and pretty terrified of Mrs. Ball, so counting on anyone coming forward on my behalf was hopeless. I swallowed hard and proceeded to bend over, placing my body downward across her lap.

Immediately, she began spanking me swat after swat using her firm, skinny hand. She really had a pretty good swing for an older, frail kind of lady. I don't recall being in a lot of pain, but my face was beet-red from embarrassment.

Finally, she swung for the last time, and the punishment was over. With tear filled eyes I looked up into the faces of my fellow classmates. The ones who dared look me in the face had an expression of guilt. Slowly, I walked back to my desk and even more slowly eased into my seat. My backside was a little extra sore than it had been before. I'm sure for the remainder of the day I heard very little that my teacher said. I was mad at her. However, I did look back later on that day and smile.

The picture that brought a smile to my face was this. There I was in last year's purple polyester dress that was a little too short on me. On my white little legs I wore black, almost knee-high rain boots. My six year-old skinny body was kicking my boots back and forth with every swat, hoping all the time my panties weren't showing because my dress was too small.

GOODNIGHT!

SLOPPY JOES

I confess I'm a very picky eater and have been all my life. I don't like to eat mayonnaise, ketchup, mustard, salad dressing, or anything else with vinegar in it. My mom, dad and grandparents who all loved me dearly allowed me to be like this. This was all fine when I was a baby, toddler, and pre-school age. I was able to eat whatever I wanted on my hamburger, hotdog, and everything else. Eating out with me was a pain, but we didn't eat out much back then anyway.

I was very anxious to turn five years old and be able to go to school. The first day of school finally arrived, and after some tears for my mom on the first day, I adjusted nicely. However, I didn't adjust well to our school lunches. In those days, not very many children packed their lunches. Also, there weren't choices of different meals. For example, if we were having hot dogs, you either ate hot dogs or starved. Starving actually would have been an option if you weren't in Mrs. Ball's first grade class. One of Mrs. Balls many rules included eating everything on our plates. Even if you weren't a picky eater, this was a huge request. The cafeteria always served strange foods that usually didn't even compare to your mom's home cooking.

Some of my favorite meals were pizza, chicken, and hamburgers. The day I always dreaded was the day we would have sloppy joes. I hated, absolutely hated sloppy joes. I don't know why I hated them so much because I had never really tasted one. Nonetheless, I had convinced myself that when they prepared them, they must have put ketchup, vinegar, and other ingredients in them that I didn't like. The unknown was probably what convinced me that I hated them.

It didn't take Mrs. Ball long to figure out that I was a picky eater. This particular day, I was sitting only four chairs down from her. As I lined up to get my lunch tray, I knew by the smell what was on the menu. I couldn't mistake the smell of sloppy joes. I could smell those disgusting things a mile away.

I lined up with the others and watched intently as the cafeteria workers prepared my tray and handed it to me. We were seated in an orderly row, and I began the familiar process of playing with my food.

A couple of my classmates who were sitting across from me asked, "Are you going to eat it?" They knew me well.

Once before when we had sloppy joes, I actually cried as I took bites and made myself sick to my stomach. Mrs. Ball had already glanced my way more than once. I would look back and try to smile. The thought of eating that sloppy joe already had my stomach churning. I slowly ate my corn and began drinking some milk. We also had mixed fruit, and I picked out the two kinds I liked and ate them.

The idea came to me as I was washing down the fruit with my milk, the best inspiration I had had in a long time. I subtly began my task. I took a bite of my sloppy joe trying desperately not to chew or taste it. Next, I picked up my milk carton, and when Mrs. Ball looked away, I quickly spit it into the milk carton. Wow! The first bite was gone, and I didn't have to stomach it. I continued my plan and was on bite number four before my friend Amy across the table caught on to what I was doing. Amy nearly burst out laughing, but quickly refrained when Mrs. Ball looked our way.

"Quiet down, girls," Mrs. Ball stated in her firm voice.

Now, nearly half our table knew I was up to something. Everyone was watching me intently, awaiting my next move. With all of this attention, I knew I could get caught, so I decided to make the next few bites much larger ones. My next bite was the biggest yet, and just as I was reaching for my milk carton, I felt someone kick my leg under the lunch table. I looked up to find Mrs. Ball looking right at me. I began to slowly chew, careful not to swallow one morsel, as I looked at her with a grin. Crash! Someone dropping his lunch tray saved me, and Mrs. Ball's quick glance in his direction gave me the second I needed. Quickly, I spit out the sloppy joe remains into my milk carton. I also took this distraction as an opportunity to pinch off two more good size pieces and shove them frantically into my milk carton.

Only two or three more bites and the whole sloppy joe would be gone. It was as if everyone in the whole cafeteria was watching me, including Mrs. Ball. I anxiously waited for another distraction, but nothing happened. The lunch half hour was almost over and Mrs. Ball had gotten out of her seat to come around and make sure we had all finished our lunch.

"You're doing good, Jamie," she admitted to me and added, "just a few more bites."

The boy next to me was released to take his tray, and when he got up, I took another bite and quickly disposed of it in my milk carton. Everyone around me was finished and getting up to empty their trays. Now with only a couple of us still eating, Mrs. Ball could really keep her eyes on us.

Her last call to finish up came, and I was determined not to eat that sloppy joe. Out of desperation I picked up the last big piece and shoved it in my mouth as I got up to empty my tray into the trash can. All eyes were on me and when I got to the trash, I turned my back to Mrs. Ball. Slowly, I spit that last bite into the trash. As I looked up, nearly all my classmates were looking at me, smiling. In their eyes I had conquered. However, I was just happy to have survived another sloppy joe lunch day.

As we lined up to go back to class, Amy asked me, "Did you actually swallow any of your sloppy joe?"

"No, not a single bite," I replied.

Mrs. Ball tapped me on the shoulder that very instant and exclaimed, "Jamie, I'm very proud of you for eating all of your lunch today."

I made no comment, but a small smile glimmered on my face.

GOODNIGHT!

BATHTIME

Our mobile home had two main doors. From the living room was a narrow hallway that led to the two bedrooms and our one bathroom. When you entered the main front door you were entering the living room and immediately to your right was our kitchen. The back door was located across the hall from our one bathroom. This back door made for a quick exit back outside to play after running in for bathroom breaks.

In the summertime when we were really little, my brother and I would usually play outside from the time we woke up until dark. Virginia summers were short, and we didn't want to miss a single moment of playing outdoors. This particular day was no different. The early morning was cool, but the day began to heat up quickly. Mitch and I played outside all morning, not coming in for a single potty break. We finally took a break to eat lunch, but were back outside as soon as we finished eating.

Some days we played out even after dark, but tonight Mom had us come in and clean up before suppertime. I was almost finished with my bath when Mitch hopped in the tub. Mom thought Mitch was old enough to take his own bath, so once I was out of the tub, she went back to washing dishes. I had plopped down in our worn comfortable rocking chair and was busy watching television.

Neither my mom nor I realized how long Mitch had been missing in action. However, a scream and hilarious laughter from outside informed us something was going on somewhere. Mom turned from the kitchen sink and looked at me and together our eyes darted to the hallway towards the bathroom. If either of us had been listening or looking, we would have already noticed the breeze coming down the hallway because the back door was wide open. We both flew towards the bathroom only to find still water and an empty tub. Mitch was nowhere in sight. The laughter was still ringing outside our back door, and as my mom dashed out the back door, I was right on her heels.

In an instant we found the reason for the first scream and the laughter. There, in the middle of the dirt road sat my one and only brother. He sat there stark naked just playing in the dirt like nothing was wrong and no one was around. His body, still wet from leaving the bathtub, was gradually taking in a little mud here and a little there in splotches. Certainly, Mitch's naked body was enough to cause laughter, but when Mom and I arrived on the scene, we realized it was more than that.

Mitch was sitting in the very center of this dirt road just outside our mobile home. He was scooping up dirt in his hands, focusing intently on making a pretend racetrack with the dirt. Dirt was on his face, in his wet blonde hair, and in patches on the rest of his body. Mitch, however, was so involved in what he was doing that he was not aware that the neighbors were all standing there laughing. Apparently, he had forgotten also that he was naked when he got out of the tub and made his way to the dirt road.

With a smile on her face, Mom said, “Mitch, what in the world do you think you’re doing?”

As he looked up at the sound of her voice, he suddenly realized several people surrounded him. He then looked down at his own naked body and said, “Oops.”

His ornery grin and laugh is probably what got him his spanking, or maybe Mom was just a little embarrassed in front of the neighbors. Mom took his arm and started swatting his little bottom. She ended up swatting him all the way back to the house. Up the steps to the back door they went and back into the tub went Mitch’s bare little body.

Mom decided to keep watch over Mitch this time and be sure he took his bath. She helped him shampoo the mud out of his hair and clean behind his ears. Mitch goofed off a little more in the tub, and Mom told him it was time to get out and dry off. While drying him off, my mom asked, “Mitch, what in the world were you thinking by going outside naked?”

My brother replied, “That’s just it Mom, I just wasn’t thinking.”

He ended up getting a smile and a hug.

GOODNIGHT!

Not exactly 'Bath Time' but Bradley, Mitch and I cooling off on a hot summer day.

MISSED SANTA AGAIN

I can't remember exactly what year it happened, but I believe I was six or seven years old. The day, however, I do remember. It was December 24, Christmas Eve. My brother Mitch and I had woken up early that morning already anxious for the night to come. Tonight, Santa Claus would be coming, and we could hardly contain our excitement. We weren't exactly sure what gifts Santa would be bringing, but we would definitely be ready.

The day seemed to drag by slowly from the very beginning. Fortunately, this December day was not as freezing cold as most, and we were able to go outside and play for a little while. We were only able to round up a couple of friends to play with because many had already left to visit relatives for Christmas Eve. My grandparents on my dad's side lived next door, and my other grandparents lived about thirty minutes away. We called them Ma and Pa Davis, and they would be visiting us tomorrow.

After playing outside for over an hour, I decided to go inside for a while. Once I was inside, I plopped down on the sofa in front of the television in hopes this would take up some time. Mitch, who could always handle the cold weather better than I, stayed outside to play with his friends longer. I warmed up pretty quick and went looking through the kitchen for something to snack on. With some cookies in one hand and a glass of milk in the other, I went back to my spot on the couch and watched television.

My relaxing moment ended abruptly, but with a nice surprise. My cousin Annette and her family stopped by for awhile to visit. Annette and I played and talked and talked and played. We were both really anxious for Santa's arrival that night. Before we knew it, two whole hours had passed and Annette and her parents were leaving to visit her other grandparents.

As I walked away from her car, waving one more good-bye, I noticed the sun was starting to go down. Darkness was creeping in, and Santa would be visiting soon. With a bounce in my step, I walked back inside knowing that it wouldn't be long now. Once inside, my mom headed for the kitchen and was removing the ham from the oven. She had already prepared the rolls, potato salad, and green beans earlier in the day. I went over to the Christmas tree and plugged in the lights, and Mitch added to the spirit by putting on an Elvis Presley Christmas album. The Christmas excitement was in the air.

Mom began to set the table, and a few minutes later Dad walked in the front door. He had been talking to our neighbor, Dickey, while Mom finished preparing the food. Supper was ready, and we all gathered around the table. My dad no sooner got the first bite in his mouth, when I blurted out, "Santa Clause is coming tonight, Daddy!"

"Sure is," my dad replied with a small grin on his face.

"I don't think he'll be coming to our house tonight," my brother announced. My smile turned instantly to a frown, but only for a moment.

"Yes, huh, he is to," I insisted. "Besides, if he doesn't, you won't get anything either," I went on to add. Both Mom and Dad got a good laugh from this.

Before long, supper was over, and I wandered over to my favorite rocking chair to sit and wait. Mom busied herself in the kitchen, and Mitch turned on the T.V. Dad had just sat down by Mitch when one of our neighbors knocked on the door and outside he went. I must have been in dreamland about twenty minutes later when the announcement came because I woke up with a start.

"My goodness!" a voice exclaimed, "What is all of this out here?"

"Santa Clause has come," Mitch shouted from in front of me. I was really awake now. Out of my chair and out the front door I ran. A crowd had gathered right in front of our trailer.

"Where?" I shouted, "Where?" I scooted my way into and around the huddle of people. The sky was almost pitch black.

"Right there!" my dad said, as he pointed up towards the sky.

"Where?" I pleaded again in panic. I could not see Santa at all. Everyone was looking and gazing toward the sky, and I couldn't see a single thing.

"Right there, Jamie!" my dad indicated as he pointed toward the moon and the glow around it. "Do you see him honey?"

I wanted so badly to see what everyone else was seeing. It seemed the harder I looked that maybe I did see something.

"That red glow must be Rudolph's nose," my dad hinted as he looked at me.

I concluded that I must have been looking in the wrong direction. I was brought back to earth with the words, "Mitch, Jamie, look!"

Well, I looked all right. When the huddle of folks moved back, there were presents piled right there in front of our trailer on the sidewalk. Santa must have left them.

Almost as quickly as I had ran outside, I started hauling the presents inside. Ma and Pa helped as well, as they had been in the huddle, too. The packages were in all shapes and sizes, and I could hardly wait to get inside and get the word to open our presents.

I didn't have to wait long. Mom and Dad were coming inside too. We gathered around in our cozy living room, and when my dad nodded his head, Mitch and I began to unwrap presents so quickly you would have thought the house was on fire. Mitch's first present was a set of toy cowboy guns and he immediately started yelling, "Pow, pow, pow!"

I saw him open a cowboy hat and that was all the attention I paid him. I was more concerned with my own gifts now. The first two gifts I opened were dolls and I squealed instantly with excitement. Next, I opened up a tea set and wanted to stop there and go put some kool-aid or something in it so I could serve everyone. Mom encouraged me to wait and finish opening the rest of my presents first. This was an awesome Christmas. My Grandma Justice helped me wrap my new dolls in blankets and then held them while I served tea. Well, actually it was kool-aid.

The night's festivities included my dad playing some of our favorite Christmas songs and other tunes on his guitar. Another Christmas had come and gone, and the presents were great. I just couldn't believe I had missed Santa again.

GOODNIGHT!

LIGHTNING BUGS

One of my favorite sights of summer was the gloriously shining lightning bugs. I was fascinated with them. I would see one of the lightning bugs light up, run toward him to catch him in my hands, and just when I thought I had him, he would disappear. He would then light up again close by and repeat his little disappearing act. These little insects certainly had a personality of their own, but I enjoyed them.

A normal summer night included a round of hide-n-seek, and this evening was no exception. My older brother, Mitch, our neighbor Bradley, and anyone else we could round up would all begin as soon as it was officially dark. We would take turns hiding and seeking each other out until one of us kept getting found first. This particular night I ended up being the first one found over and over. Part of the reason I kept getting caught first was my hiding in the same places over and over. The other reason had to do with me jumping up to try to catch a lightning bug at the wrong time.

We played for over an hour, and then Bradley and the other kids had to go in for the night. Mitch and I had a few more minutes to play outside, so I convinced him to help me catch some lightning bugs to bring inside. He agreed, and I quickly ran inside to find an old pickle jar to use. I got Mitch to poke some holes in the top of it, and we began our search. We were off and running, trying to see who could catch the most lightning bugs to put in our jar. We actually thought this would be an easy task. The lightning bug would light up, we would have our eyes right on him, and presto—he was cupped in our hands. But when we would look inside our cupped hands for our little flying friend, he would be gone. We began to figure out that the instant his light went out he plummeted through the air.

Finally, Mitch and I outsmarted a few and our little jar was starting to light up. Actually, when Mom yelled for us to come in we were on a pretty good roll, catching one every few minutes.

Mitch decided he would hide the jar behind his back and not let Mom see it when we came inside. I'm not sure why he did this because she didn't mind us catching and keeping the little bugs anyway. I went along with his little game, and he snuck past Mom to our bedroom and put the jar under my bottom bunk.

Bath time was next, and of course, we needed one more snack and drink before bedtime. Ten o'clock was the usual summer bedtime, and we had already exceeded that a little. Mom came in and told us goodnight and tucked us in. We both had a silly grin on our face, and Mom noticed.

"What are you two up to?" she said.

We answered in unison, "Nothing!"

Mom smiled back at us then kissed us goodnight. Mitch and I waited less than a minute after she left before we found our lightning bug jar and got it out. We loved watching them go on and off in our dark room. Actually, it was quite amazing how much light they made all together. Our eyes were kind of getting dizzy as they were lighting up in unison in that old pickle jar. There must have been fifteen or twenty in there. I don't remember who started giggling first, but one of us did, and Mom came back in our room.

"So, this is what you two were grinning about earlier," she said with a smile, as she glanced at our jar of lightning bugs. "Well, its bedtime you two," she said smiling, "I think I'll take this pickle jar with me."

Mom took the jar, and we realized we were pretty tired anyway. We giggled a few more minutes after she left and then went straight to sleep.

When I woke the next morning and rolled over I noticed the pickle jar on our dresser. Mom must have brought it back to our room after we fell asleep. There wasn't any movement, and I slowly walked over to the dresser.

Mitch startled me when he said, "What are you doing?"

As I jerked around I replied, "I think our bugs didn't pay their light bill." We gave each other a brief smile as we headed off to the kitchen for breakfast.

GOODNIGHT!

Mitch and I on a typical 'Snow Day'

SNOW DAY

Growing up in Virginia was a kid's dreamland in the winter. We would take our baths at night, lay out our school clothes, and Mom would tuck us in snuggly on winter nights. The sky would be clear, yet many times while we slept our little town would get covered with glorious inches of snow. We would wake up and know instantly by the temperature of our little two-bedroom mobile home that the weather had changed. I was always the early riser, and as I crawled out of bed, the glare would hit me like a jolt. I would go towards the window and know in an instant... "Snow day!"

On one such day, our entire yard was completely covered in an icy white blanket of snow. I woke up my brother and turned on the radio to wait for the official announcement. Our shouts of joy sounded out as the radio announcers voice said those words every kid in Richlands, Virginia wanted to hear. "Also, schools will be closed today in Tazewell County," the announcer would say. I wasn't quite sure what living in Tazewell County meant, but I knew we were part of it.

We were instantly jumping with joy. Our mom and dad still had to go to work, but Grandma lived next door, and the best sled-riding hill in the neighborhood was right by her house. I can only remember the city workers closing off that hill a couple of times, and today ended up being one of those times. The straight down slope was so packed with snow-turned-ice that even cars with chains couldn't handle it. When we saw those bright orange cones blocking off traffic, we were shouting all the more. This meant we could go up and down all day and not need to worry about the cars.

Ma and Pa Justice, our babysitters for the day, insisted we have a big breakfast before we headed out to play in the snow. They were both great cooks. Pa started frying the bacon and eggs while Grandma made biscuits and her famous homemade white gravy. I loved Grandma's white gravy on my biscuits. The smell was wonderful, and we ate heartily.

We bundled up from head to toe and started rounding up our friends. Bradley, who was my age, was the first to join us. Next, we knocked on Theresa's door, and she said she would be out soon. By the time we pulled our sleds out of the shed and made it to the level part of the top of the hill, other kids were gathering.

I'm not sure how my brother Mitch talked me into it, but somehow he got to go first. Bradley and Theresa went together next while I was waiting on Mitch to bring our sled back up the hill. Theresa looked back at me smiling as she yelled, "Come on, Jamie, you're going to love it!"

I hopped on and, being three years younger than Mitch, chickened out on going by myself. Mitch hopped on with me, which just intensified the ride. A little push, and we went soaring down the hill, me screaming all the way. Mitch grabbed the front end of the sled as we neared the bottom and made a quick turn to the left. We both went flying off the sled, Mitch landing on me. He laughed his goofy laugh and after giving him a dirty look, I couldn't hold back a grin myself. It was going to be an awesome day.

Before long our little group had grown to about fifteen kids. This was undoubtedly the best snow day ever. One of our first contests was to see whose sled could go the farthest distance once it landed at the bottom of the hill. To go the farthest at the bottom, you had to be going pretty fast coming down the hill. After two rides with my brother and the speed of the sled, I decided to go alone. Mitch was a lot of fun, but slightly crazy when it came to things like this. We all got two tries to see who could go the farthest, and a boy named Michael from two blocks over won.

Next, we decided to have the craziest rider contest. Mitch went down backwards. I just laid down backwards on my stomach for my crazy ride. Our neighbor Bradley screamed all the way down, and the other kids all did various silly stunts. Mitch, of course, was not to be outdone. He decided to begin his ride standing up on the sled. He was only standing for a second or two before plopping down to finish his ride. We were all impressed, though, and he won the crazy ride vote.

About that time Grandma called us in to warm up with some hot chocolate. If we were cold, we didn't know it, but the words hot chocolate got our attention. Ma and Pa were the best. They invited the whole gang of us inside, and after we drank and thawed out about twenty minutes, we were back at it.

I'm not sure where we got our energy to keep lugging our sleds up the steep, slippery hill, but we did. The only other break we took that afternoon was for lunch. Everyone took a fairly long lunch break and warmed up real good. By two-thirty that afternoon we all went back to the hill, and at about four o'clock, some parents started getting off work and we had an audience for ourselves. We really began to show off then. Mitch did his crazy stand up ride, and I even rode with him and four others in a pile-up. Our pile-up on the sled ended in a pile-up at the bottom of the hill as well when we crashed. We had a blast.

All too soon, two policemen arrived, removing the orange cones and once again allowing traffic through our street. This ended our snow day sled riding, but we all went to our separate homes very content. It had been a great day of fun. It had been a Virginia Snow Day.

GOODNIGHT!

ROCK FIGHT

Looking back, I can't remember who's idea it was to have a rock fight in the first place. I'd like to blame my brother Mitch, but the idea could have been my own. Naturally, our neighborhood friends all thought having a rock fight was a great idea.

As in all neighborhood games, we decided to have two leaders choose teams. Ironically, Mitch led one side and I was the captain of the other. The choosing process began, and I chose mostly boys because I felt they would throw farther than the girls. Our intent, of course, was for this to be safe, clean fun. One strange thing about being a child is you never really think about the ending. Having a rock fight seemed to be a good idea for a boring summer day, and none of us really thought about how the game might end.

Mitch, of course, felt he had the better team, but I didn't mind. We each split up and went to gather as many rocks as we could find. Some we found were very small and others were quite large. A designated area was chosen to make our pile, and in a matter of minutes we had plenty and were ready to begin. Mitch chose one side of the gravel road we lived on, and my team took the opposite side.

Each team gathered plywood, but my team also found a few broken cinder blocks to use as barricades. We worked together assembling our barricades, which would only protect a few kids. Anyone who was not sitting right behind the barricade would be an easy target. Finally, our fort made of cinder block and plywood was in place and everyone was ready to begin. Mitch decided that on the count of three our rock war would begin. We would only stop if a car came by or when we ran out of rocks.

"One, Two, Three!" We all shouted, and the rock war began.

Mitch was right in the front of his barricade on his team, and I was in about the same place on my side. Rocks were flying one by one back and forth. Each of us ducked when we saw a rock coming our direction. Half the rocks their team threw didn't even make it to our barricade, and the same was true with many of the ones we threw also.

All was going great with only an occasional hit by a tiny stone that would only sting for a minute. Both teams were dodging, throwing, laughing and having the time of their lives. One of the last joyful things I remember about our rock war was my brother Mitch's big toothy grin. I obviously got such a good look at his grin that I didn't notice the rock he was throwing directly at me. Smack! I was hit right in the forehead. Not only was I hit, but I was also screaming. As quickly as our war had begun, it had ended. No one panicked at first, but when the blood started streaming down my face everyone was really scared, especially me. Two of my teammates went running toward our house for help.

I distinctly remember looking straight back at Mitch only to see his big grin replaced by a look of horror and shock. He was truly concerned—either for me or for himself. Since he was the one who threw the rock that hit his sister, he definitely had some explaining to do. At any rate, he came to my rescue, bringing his teammates with him.

My mom soon arrived on the scene, but things had gotten slightly worse. The lump on my head was not only bleeding, but also swelling. Along with my bleeding was black grime from where the dirt from my hands and my tears had mixed. She didn't even ask what had happened, but quickly escorted me to our mobile home.

When we walked in the kitchen door, Mom went right to work. She applied wet cloths to my head to wash away the blood and dirt so she could see how bad the hit really was. Once she washed the dirt off, my mom could see that the rock had broken the skin and the swelling was about the size of a small egg. Fortunately, there wasn't a deep gash so at least I wasn't going to need stitches or anything. Still not asking for details, Mom bandaged me up and told Mitch and me to go take our baths.

We obeyed. Neither of us was sure what she might be thinking. We decided to linger as long as possible in the tub, just in case we were in trouble when we got out. Mitch and I both took our time getting dressed, and before long it was time for supper. Our mom was extremely quiet during the meal and didn't once mention what had happened. Normally, we would be in some really big trouble for something like this, so Mom's behavior was really strange.

After dinner, we plopped down to watch some television, assuming all was going to be okay. The suspense ended about an hour later when our dad arrived home from work. Mom had stored up all her thoughts and feelings about our rock fight and told it all to Dad. She explained how we were throwing rocks across the road and could have hit a car. “One of those rocks could have put out another child’s eye,” she went on to tell Dad.

Mitch and I chose that moment to go find a good hiding place. Mitch found a place behind the couch, and I hid behind the rocking chair. The hiding places were slim in our two-bedroom mobile home.

Finally, Mom had her say and Dad decided his supper could wait a few more minutes. Dad found Mitch first and although he only got eight licks, by the way he was screaming, you would have thought he got a hundred. I actually thought for a few brief moments that since I had been injured I wasn’t going to get a spanking too. Well, my dad had other ideas. The issue wasn’t who got hurt, but the fact that we were having a rock fight. My dad easily found me hiding behind the chair.

“Come on out here,” he demanded. I did, and within a matter of seconds I was crying again. This time it wasn’t my head that was hurting, but the other end. I ended up with a double dose that day.

Looking back, I’d say we could have just played a game of tag, hide-n-seek, or certainly something else.

GOODNIGHT!

KING OF THE MOUNTAIN

My earliest memory ever includes Bradley living next door. Bradley was the same age as me. However, we were never mistaken for twins or even siblings. Bradley had big brown eyes and dark black hair. I, on the other hand, had blue eyes and blonde hair.

We both lived in mobile homes. In fact, Bradley's mobile home was only about two cars length from mine. I could be in his yard in seconds and at his front door in less than a minute. Bradley's mobile home was located on a double lot, and at the top of the empty lot was a totally awesome hill.

We were always coming up with fun things to do with Bradley's hill. When the wheels weren't broken on our wagon, we'd hop in it and take turns riding it down Bradley's hill. Occasionally, we might play pirate ship and use the top of the hill as a lookout for any enemy ships. However, the best game we ever played there was "King of the Mountain." Of course, as the title suggests, there had to be a King and the King would reign at the top of the mountain, or in our case, Bradley's hill. The object was for the King to be in power at the top of the hill. He could keep that position as long as no one could pull him down. As soon as someone pulled him off from the top area of the hill, that person was now King. We would all then go back to the bottom of the hill and start over making our way up the hill trying to catch whoever was King off guard.

We would usually take turns regarding who would be the first King for that day. Most often Bradley talked us into letting him be King first since the hill was in his yard. Also, Bradley wasn't very big and strong like some of the other kids, so he knew he might not get to be King once the game started. This particular day Bradley was King first. Mitch, Bradley, and I were all ready to start when John and his sister Jenny showed up. "The more the merrier," we said, and the game began.

I was the first to make my way to the top, but Bradley pushed me away, which meant I was back at the bottom starting over again. My brother Mitch, who was three years older and much bigger than Bradley, was the next to grab Bradley and of course he was off the throne. Mitch became the new King.

Mitch was the biggest of all us kids playing so the key was to wear him down. There were four of us, and one of Mitch. Johnny was the first to grab Mitch, however he was unsuccessful and down he came. Bradley was right behind him going up the hill and quickly came tumbling down the hill. Jenny and I decided to make our attack together. However, Mitch's strength just pushed us right back where we started from.

John was only one year younger than Mitch, just not as big. He was next up, but Mitch had him rolling down the hill in seconds. For the next twenty minutes we would charge up the hill, grab hold of King Mitch and yet down again we would go. We all thought by now he would be getting tired and surely one of us would get to be King for a while. Unfortunately, we were the ones who were getting tired.

With Mitch on top gloating and all of us at the bottom exhausted, Bradley got a great idea. We all gathered in a huddle as he shared his brainstorm idea with us. He ended up having to tell us three times, since Mitch was yelling, "Hey look, I'm King of the Mountain. I'm King. I'm King."

Finally, through Mitch's yelling we were able to hear Bradley's plan. We would slowly crawl up the mountain, each one of us taking a different angle. We would move slowly and at the same speed to keep our King guessing. The plan involved us moving slowly, then fast, then slow again, so Mitch couldn't watch all four of us at once. We would continue this to the edge of the top, since Mitch could only cast us off once we made it to the edge. Then, Johnny was going to shout out, "Now!" and all four of us were going to grab his ankles at the same time. This quick movement would hopefully take him off his throne. Only one of us could actually be King, but we didn't care. All we knew was that it was time for King Mitch to come off the mountain.

As we got down on our tummies to crawl up the mountain, Mitch began his goofy laugh, "Ha, ha, ha, oh I'm being attacked by crawling creatures!" he shouted.

We didn't care. We had a plan and were going for it. We were acting out our plan perfectly, and Mitch had quit laughing and was starting to look a little concerned. Two of us would crawl slowly while the other two would crawl quickly. We did this back and forth to keep him guessing. Mitch was looking to his right, then left, then in front and behind. If nothing else, we had him wondering. Jenny was moving a little faster than the rest of us, so we had to quickly play catch up. Before we knew it, we were at the edge of the top and at that instant John shouted, "Now!"

Quickly, two of us grabbed one of his ankles, while the other two latched onto his other one. With one hard pull he was over the hill and on his way down. John ran to the top, and we gladly let him.

"Hey, Mitch, look who's King now?" John gloated.

Mitch laughed his goofy laugh and said, "Okay, okay, I guess you guys pulled one over on the old King."

He then looked up the hill at John and said, "Enjoy Johnny boy, cause the Ol' King is coming back to take his throne."

Mitch made his way up the hill with all of us behind him, and our game continued.

GOODNIGHT!

CHRISTMAS TREE HILL

In my earlier years, we lived in an area called 'The Brickyard' because an industry where bricks were made was within walking distance of my home. My Grandpa Justice worked there. This was a good job for him because he could walk to work. My grandpa never drove his whole life, and neither did my grandma. My grandma cleaned the offices there so she could easily walk to her job at the Brickyard, too.

Around the bend from the brickyard was a winding road that led up a very steep hill. At the very top of this narrow steep hill, there was a giant frame of a Christmas tree covered with multi-colored Christmas lights. Every year at Christmas, the lights would be turned on and they could be seen from the distance throughout our neighborhood and town. Every year my brother and I looked forward to the night we would look up and see the lighted tree.

This particular year was no different. Every time we were out driving around at night, we would stretch our necks to see the glorious tree. One Friday night, just after dark, my dad looked at my brother and me and said, "Anyone want to drive up the Christmas Tree Hill and get a closer look?"

"I do!" We shouted in unison. We were up fast as lightening, grabbing our coats and putting on our shoes. We were out the door and in the back seat of the car in no time flat.

We could hardly wait for our dad and mom to come out the front door. We lived very close to Christmas Tree Hill, so we would be there in just a few minutes. There was still some snow on the ground, but for the most part the roads were clear. At least, the main roads were clear. We were traveling the main roads for a while, and Dad had just turned on the narrow winding road that would lead us up the hill and to the Christmas tree.

As soon as our journey led up the winding road, our dad slowed down his speed drastically. It was exciting and scary all at the same time. We were traveling around and around like a spiral staircase. All seemed to be going well when all of a sudden our little car slipped. I gasped and Mitch laughed. He thought this was so exciting. Dad continued on, slowly winding around curve after curve. I heard Mom tell him once or twice under her breath that maybe we should try to come back when the roads weren't so icy. Dad's reply both times was, "Don't worry, we'll be fine."

I tended to side with my mom, but I could see Dad was going for it anyway. We only had about three more trips around the winding road and we would be at the top. Our car was slowly creeping now, sliding backwards occasionally. Mitch and I had taken our minds off the roads now and were looking up excitedly as our Christmas Tree Hill tree came closer and closer in view. The tree was enormous, and the lights were out of this world. Every color imaginable was sparkling on that tree, and it stood taller and wider than any we had ever seen.

Mitch and I were so caught up in staring at the tree that we didn't even realize we were circling the last bend and would be on the top in a matter of seconds. In an instant, we were there. Dad parked right in front of the tree, and we just sat in our car for quite awhile admiring the lights. At last we got out of the car and looked around our little town of Richlands. We felt like we were on top of the world. It was so cool.

Since it had taken longer to drive up there than Dad anticipated, we were only able to stay and enjoy the scenery about thirty minutes. It was then time to begin our journey down the winding road. Reluctantly, Mitch and I got back in the car, and Dad began to turn our car around on the narrow, steep hill we were on. First he backed up, and then went forward, repeating this several times. The last attempt before we would be on our way turned out to be a series of events I will never forget. Our car started sliding out of control, and my dad was barely able to get control of it before we were at the edge of Christmas Tree Hill. As I peered out the window, I saw that we were on the extreme edge. One more move in the wrong direction and we were going over the side of the hill. My mom, brother, and I were all holding our breath as Dad went from reverse to drive and back again, while pressing on the emergency break.

"Mom, I'm scared," I whimpered as I looked at her for reassurance.

"It's okay." She replied in a not-so-certain voice. "Just be quiet."

Being quiet while your whole life flashed in front of your eyes was certainly easier said than done. Dad was working frantically to keep control of our vehicle, and although I could only see the back of his head, I knew he was panicking, too. Part of me wanted to lean to one side of the car or the other in hopes this might help. Even my brother Mitch, who would normally love this kind of excitement, was turning pale.

The silence was broken when we heard the back end slip and thump over the bank. Mitch and I screamed before we finally heard my dad's voice.

"Don't anyone move, not one muscle. I need to think a minute," he said.

One move in the wrong direction and we were going over the hill. I was brought back to reality when Dad said my name.

"Jamie, I need you to very slowly move to the front seat," my dad said in a quiet, but stern voice.

I wanted to ask about Mitch, but I knew this wasn't the time for questions. With slow, direct movements, I crawled out of the back seat and went right to my mom's lap. She held me tight as she looked towards the back seat at Mitch.

"Mitch," my dad spoke.

"Yes?" my brother answered.

"In just a minute, I want you to slowly climb into my seat, and as you do, I'll be opening my door and getting out of the car," Dad said.

None of us were exactly sure what the plan was. All we knew for sure was that our car was hanging in the balance, and we were in it. While my thoughts wandered, my dad spoke again.

"Now, Mitch!" Dad announced.

They were both instantly in action. As Dad pushed on his door, we could feel movement. We knew we had slipped a little more backwards. All was still in seconds, and Mitch was now behind the wheel. I was even hesitant to move my head, but out of the corner of one eye, I saw my dad motion for Mitch to roll down the window. Our dad then moved towards the back end of the car.

He spoke again, "Mitch, when I push, steer sharply to the right, because we need to get this one tire on some solid ground for traction."

My dad pushed and Mitch steered, and nothing happened. Again and again Dad pushed, but we were still in the same place. I could tell Mitch was panicking by the way the side of his face was looking flushed. My mom was breathing hard, and we all knew Dad had to be getting tired. With all these thoughts swimming in my head, I suddenly felt a thump. I knew it was all over. This was it. We were goners. I closed my eyes and prepared to die. Mitch's voice brought me back to reality.

"Good going Dad, we made it," he said.

"Okay, son, hop in the back, and let's get out of here," my dad announced.

We were safe. Whew! The thump I felt was our tire on solid ground again. I hugged my mom one more time, and crawled back to my seat. Our little car was still sliding a little, but we all knew the worst was over and we were on our way down the hill.

I turned around and looked back up at the Christmas tree as we drove down the winding roads. In my chatty voice I said, "We certainly saw the Christmas Tree on Christmas Tree Hill tonight."

My mom and dad both got a good laugh out of this.

"We certainly did!" They said in unison.

It was a good thing we had taken a good look at that tree because we never drove up Christmas Tree Hill again.

GOODNIGHT!

FISH GUTS

My daddy loved to fish, and he was good at it. We could fish all day, and I'd barely get a nudge on my hook, while my dad reeled in fish after fish. Trout was a familiar meal at our house.

Sometimes my dad would clean the fish at the river, but most of the time the cleaning took place at our home. My cousin, Annette, and I were playing in the front yard with some of my friends when dad drove in from his fishing adventure that day. We both went running toward the car.

"Did you catch any?" I asked, even though I already knew the answer. My dad always caught some.

"You'll see," he said, as he opened the cooler for us.

"Wow!" exclaimed Annette, as she viewed the cooler more than half full of fish. We were definitely having a fish fry tonight. Dad picked up the cooler and headed towards the house. Occasionally, Dad would clean them outside, or ask Mom to do this messy job. Today, however, he was doing the honors himself. Dad brought the bucket of fish right into our small trailer kitchen. One by one he took them off the line they had earlier been strung on and began piling them in our kitchen sink. For me, this was great fun, but of course, I wasn't getting my hands dirty. My dad would take the fish, one at a time, and place them on a cutting board. He positioned the cutting board on the countertop right beside our kitchen sink. Dad would pull out his trusty pocketknife, and off would go the head. Dad would just kind of flip it over in the sink, and there's where he started his pile of fish remains.

Once the head was off, he took an object similar to a pot scraper and scaled the fish. Basically, he would take the scraper up and down the fish's body, scraping off the scales into the sink. Next, he carefully opened up the fish insides, which was kind of like cutting rubber. Well, everything that fish had eaten in the last day or so came oozing out. This was a disgusting sight. Next, Dad would use his same pocketknife and scoot all those guts and stuff into the sink with the fish head. Dad would put his finished fish on ice until suppertime and pick the next one up for the slaughter.

This particular day had been a good catch day for my dad. I can't remember if there were twelve, fifteen or maybe even more in there, but there were a lot. One by one went their heads, then they were gutted, and the remains kept piling up in the kitchen sink. Finally, the last fish was done, and Mom would start the frying soon.

Getting rid of the insides and heads was next. Dad took an old, empty bread bag and started picking up the guts and heads with his bare hands. He put them inside the plastic bread bag handful by handful. Taking out the full bag of fish guts was a common chore for me at age eight. I heard him call my name, and I ran to the door to get the bag. Dad handed the bread bag to me after he had tied it securely shut. I was supposed to take the bag and throw it over the side of the fence. Usually, the neighborhood cats would feast on the remains later.

I had the bag in my hand and was anxious to get rid of it so I could go back to playing with my cousin Annette. Annette had come over to our house to play and spend the night.

"What ya got?" she yelled, as I headed out the door.

"Fish guts," I replied, "Want some?"

She screamed, and I proceeded on towards the fence to get rid of the smelly bag. Being a normal kid, I couldn't just give one giant swing and throw the bag over the fence. I decided to build up some momentum and speed. First, I did the swirl thing with the bag, making it go around and around. Then I would let it spin the other way, sort of like a yo-yo would. Next, I thought I would try the side-to-side swing, left, then right, left, then right. I probably would have continued this for a few more minutes, but my cousin Annette's shout of "You're it!" got my attention. Finally remembering that we were in the middle of a game of tag when my dad called motivated me to complete my mission. With all the strength I had, I began to swing the bag around and around in a ferris wheel motion. What happened next left me stunned. Without any warning the bottom of the bag split wide open, and fish guts went flying.

Instead of the whole bag going over the fence in front of me, the bag busted open behind me. I quickly looked up to find Annette covered from head to toe with fish guts. There were even a couple of the heads lying motionless on top of her head. The rest of the fish guts were scattered all over her body. There were parts on her legs, down her arms, and even some lying on her shoulders. Her shirt was disgusting, but probably the worst part was her face. Some pieces had landed on her cheek, and there was a little strand hanging out one of her nostrils. Annette could barely keep one of her eyes open as something was oozing off one eyelid. She was standing there holding her arms out in a helpless position crying something that sounded like "Uh…Uh…Uh…Uh." My friends and I wanted to help, but the sight of her caused everyone who had been playing nearby to burst out in laughter. We laughed and we looked and we realized she needed help, but what could we do without touching her? I'm not sure how long we stood there bewildered and laughing uncontrollably. Finally, Mom came outside, and the look on her face told us we were in trouble. I quickly explained that it was an accident.

"Accident or not," my mom shouted, "Help your cousin Annette get that stuff off of her." The next few minutes were spent pulling the remains out of her hair and off her back and arms. We removed the pieces stuck to her eyelash and the one near her nostril. We hadn't bargained for pieces to be inside the crevices of her ear, but they were there nonetheless. It was awful.

We finally picked all the yuk off of her, but the smell was still horrible. We took her clothes and threw them in the trash, and Mom informed the crowd of kids from the neighborhood that the party was over and to head home. My mom, Annette and I went inside and straight for the bathroom. I remember walking past my dad, and I'm sure I saw him grin. Two baths and four hair shampoos later, Annette began to look and smell like her old self again. By this time it was near bedtime, and we began preparing ourselves for bed. Up to this point, she still had not wanted to talk about it or have any of us so much as crack a smile about what had happened. This was hard because, although it was a horrible thing, it was also horribly funny. We readied ourselves for bed and sat down to have some popcorn that Mom had popped for us. I let Annette choose a T.V. show. She certainly deserved it after the day she had been through. She was still very quiet, only barely smiling when a joke was told on the show we were watching. The show was over, and we were off to brush our teeth. We went to my room, and Mom tucked us in.

The lights were finally out, and I was on the top bunk with Annette on the bottom. We talked a little, then the room got quiet for a few minutes. I was the first to break the silence, "Annette," I whispered.

"Yes," she whispered back.

In a not so quiet voice I said, "Uh…Uh…Uh…Uh." We both burst out laughing. The fish gut episode finally had a humorous ending, even for the victim.

GOODNIGHT!

Annette holding a catch of her own.

My dad with a catch of his own.

THE CAGE

I've always loved the time of year when the carnival came to town. In my hometown, few people ever went to an amusement park or Disney World, so the carnival once a year was big stuff.

This summer was like many others. We would be driving through town, and there it was, going up piece by piece. The anticipation in our hearts started rising. We would be going to the carnival soon. Since our family lived on a tight budget, we would wait for a certain night with great ticket prices to go. This year, Thursday night was the best night, and my mom said my brother and I could each invite one friend to go with us. Thursday was three days away, and I knew they would be the longest three days of my summer.

My grandma ended up inviting my brother Mitch and me over to spend the night Tuesday, so before we knew it, Wednesday was upon us. We arrived home late Wednesday morning. By the time we had lunch and finished our chores, it was late afternoon and the day was almost over.

I woke up early Thursday morning with a smile gleaming on my face. Tonight when Mom got home from work, we were going to the carnival. I jumped out of bed and ran down the hallway to look at the clock. The clock reading only 9:00 a.m. meant we had ten whole hours to wait. Certainly these would be ten very long hours. I poured myself some cereal, and while I was eating, someone knocked at the door. Our neighbor Pat wanted me to come outside to play. I quickly dressed and went outside.

Pat and I rounded up a few more friends and before we knew it, we were having a great time playing kick-ball. The games lasted until after noon and we all went our separate ways to have lunch. I fixed a peanut butter and jelly sandwich and some chicken noodle soup. Just as I was finishing slurping my soup, I noticed the clock read 1:15. Maybe this day wouldn't last forever after all. My brother Mitch showed up about that time. He had been across the creek playing with some buddies. He asked me to make him some lunch. Normally, I would have said no, but my spirits were high today so I agreed. Besides, what else did I really have to do except wait?

With lunch over and the kitchen clean, I decided to plop down and watch some television. This didn't last long because every channel was a different soap opera. I had been hoping for a cartoon. I took the time to go choose something to wear that night to the carnival. This took even less time, and it was now 2:30.

About that time I heard some commotion going on outside. I headed outside and realized Pat and two of her brothers had found a frog. I wanted to check him out for myself so outside I went. I'm amazed at how long we managed to amuse ourselves with one small frog.

Our little green friend would hop one way, and we'd follow. Then he would sit still for several minutes. We all circled him, watching and waiting for his next move. This must have gone on for hours because when I finally had to take a bathroom break, I looked at the clock and it was almost 4:30 p.m.

That was close enough for me. With excitement in my step, I went inside to get cleaned up for the carnival. I heard the front door shut just as I got out of the tub and knew my mom was home. Mitch came in seconds later and we were all bustling about getting ready. Mitch's friend, Steven, showed up, and then my friend Kim arrived a few minutes later. Within a matter of minutes, we were in the car and on our way.

The excitement escalated the closer we drove toward the carnival. With the carnival now in view, we were all beside ourselves with enthusiasm. The long line for parking didn't even put a damper on our excitement. We were parked and walking toward that glorious smell of cotton candy before we knew it.

Mitch and his friend could go off alone because they were both thirteen years old. However, Kim and I would have to hang with my mom. Kim and I went right for the Ferris wheel and quickly got on board. It was a blast. Next, Kim insisted we ride the tilt-a-whirl so my mom would ride with us. Our turn came and we had a wonderful ride. We made my mom sit in the middle so every way we turned we were leaning toward her. She loved it.

Kim and I were both anxious to play a game and try to win a stuffed animal. We tried the penny toss and did win a little toy. Next, we played the fish bowl game. We would toss a ping-pong ball toward the fish bowl. If the ball landed inside the bowl, we would win a fish. I think my mom must have had her fingers crossed when I threw because I didn't even come close. Kim, however, landed hers inside the bowl the first time. Of course, my mom got the privilege of carrying around the fish Kim had won. We were having a great time. Kim and I enjoyed most of the same rides.

Finally, we caught up with Mitch and his friend Steven. They were waiting in line at the cage ride. "Come on!" Mitch yelled to us.

I looked at Kim, and she looked at me.

"Want to?" she suggested. I was very hesitant. The cage was similar to a ferris wheel, except you were secured in a red cage that turned completely upside down. Everyone knew this could happen at the very top of the ride while others boarded down below.

"Sure," I murmured, not wanting to be the scaredy cat.

We got in the line with about twenty others and anxiously waited our turn. My stomach was churning as we got closer and closer to being the next to board the ride. The wild screams here and there didn't help my fears any. I could just envision one of those cages breaking loose as it swung around and around. These and other thoughts of the ride getting stuck on the top with us in the cage were whirling through my mind.

The two kids in front of us decided to get out of line at the last minute. Without any warning we were being secured in our cage, and the door shut.

"Give us a spin!" Kim shouted, and the carnival guy did. This is the moment my screaming began.

As our cage began to go up to the next stopping place, my screams subsided a little. Before I knew it the new riders were all on board and we were going around and around. This would have been exciting enough for me, but in addition, we were also constantly turning upside down as well. At this point I started screaming uncontrollably and with full force. "Ah, Ah, Ah!" I would scream and then I would plead, "Help, help, please let me out of here!" When all of this got me no response, I just screamed all the louder, "Ah, Ah, Ah, Ah!" Next, I screamed out, "Please, I'm getting sick!" This finally got their attention. Screaming was one thing, but my throwing up in the cage would be quite another. The ride began to slow down and stopped at our cage.

The carnival guy in charge of the cage opened our cage, looked me right in the eye, and said, "Little girl do you want off?" They had rescued me. I could finally get off this crazy ride and set my feet on solid ground. I should have been jumping with joy and running off the ride. Instead, I found myself saying something totally bizarre.

"Well, no, I guess not."

He looked at me with ultimate shock and then opened his mouth to reply, "Then stop your screaming!"

"Okay," I responded, very calmly.

He carefully closed the door to our cage. We were again going around and around and upside down. I did wish a couple of times that I had taken him up on his offer and gotten out of the cage. However, I knew better than to start screaming again.

GOODNIGHT!

NIGHTCRAWLERS

In my hometown in the hills of Virginia, one thing that was usually plentiful was night crawlers. For any of you city folk that might be reading this, a night crawler is a big, fat, juicy worm.

My dad fished a lot so hunting our own night crawlers was a way of life. Stopping and buying your fish bait from a store was something for sophisticated people to do, but not us down to earth home folk.

We were planning a fishing trip for the end of the week. My Grandma and Grandpa Justice would both be going, along with my brother, my dad, and me. Dad had just a few night crawlers left from his last fishing trip, but not near enough for what we needed. To get some easy to catch night crawlers, we needed a good Virginia rain. On Wednesday of that week, the rain began to fall in bucket size portions during the afternoon. By suppertime the rain had lightened up a little.

My grandpa and I were the explorers. We both had a way of getting a hold of those slimy little critters and pulling them right out of the ground. Tonight was going to be the perfect night. I could hardly wait as the light began to dim in the sky and darkness set in. My grandpa, or Pa as I called him, said that it was always good to wait until an hour or two after dark. My pa was right, too, because when we got out there looking, they were just lying on the ground everywhere.

I was sitting beside my grandma on the couch when the announcement came.

"Okay, girl," my grandpa said. "Let's go find us some night crawlers."

I was up in a flash and grabbing my jacket. Pa was about four steps ahead of me, but I was on his heels in no time flat. Pa and I went out the back door to get our buckets that were already waiting half full of fresh dirt. Next, Pa reached into his pocket and handed me a flashlight as he pulled his from the hanging shelf.

Knowing how much I loved to talk, Pa turned around and reminded me to be quiet. I've never understood why because I have never seen a single night crawler with ears. Nevertheless, with my lips sealed, I tiptoed quietly behind Pa.

Pa's back yard was very small. However, we would begin there first, and work our way over to my yard next door. Pa got the first one, as I knew he would, but I was right behind him with another one. Sometimes they would just be lying there with their whole bodies spread out, and other times about one half of their bodies would be hidden in the hole. The ones lying out almost appeared as if they were moonlight bathing under the stars. Of course, their relaxing moment ended quickly as the flashlight shone on them, and Pa and I jerked them up.

I would usually reach down and gather them up and put them one by one in the bucket. I learned to be quiet and fast. Often I could see five or six at a time. When I would reach down for one, the others would scurry back in their holes. Occasionally I would get two of them, but usually just one.

This particular night we were raking them in. Once we had searched an area for a few minutes, the night crawlers would start to be hesitant to come out. The ones just lying out on the ground were becoming fewer. When I would find one halfway sticking out of his hole, the tug of war would begin. Not only were they big and fat, but also slimy. Sometimes I couldn't even get a good grip. I would start to pull while the worm was trying to slide back in his hole, and the tug of war would continue. He would be winning, and then I would. Many a night crawler slipped through my grasp and back into his hole. Once in awhile we would both lose. I would be pulling and he would be struggling, and snap—his body would break in half. This was always a disgusting sight. The half he had and the half I had wasn't doing either of us any good.

With both mine and Pa's yards canvassed pretty good, we walked over to my friend Bradley's yard. We planned to continue our search there. We were finding just as many night crawlers in Bradley's yard as we had in mine.

Well, Pa and I hunted the better part of an hour that night and came in with full buckets. When we got back to the porch, we turned our flashlights on each other's piles and were very proud of ourselves. All the night crawlers were squirming around trying to figure out where they were. For now they were in our buckets, but soon they would be on a fishing pole hook.

As Pa and I were putting our buckets securely in a corner on the porch, we noticed how nasty our hands looked. Our fingernails were going to need to be cleaned really well because of handling the worms and dirt, but it was worth it.

"How was the hunt?" my grandma asked, while we were washing our hands.

"Real good," I replied.

With the night crawlers secure in their buckets, we were ready to call it a night. We were now prepared for our fishing trip and ready for a good night's rest, too.

GOODNIGHT!

My Mom and I

SURPRISE SUPPER

My parents divorced when I was nine years old. Although my dad sent monthly checks to my mom, money was still very tight. In order to make ends meet, Mom started working overtime at her job. She worked at a pajama factory called Eastern Isles. She would work 7:00 am to 3:00 pm and come home for a few hours. Around 6:00 pm, many times she would go back to work until nine or ten o'clock at night and was paid overtime pay for these hours. In addition to her job at Eastern Isles, she sold Avon products and made Raggedy Ann and Andy dolls to sell. My mom was a very hard worker, and I really wanted to do something special to help her.

One afternoon, I decided to surprise her by having dinner ready when she arrived home. I loved pizza and I knew she liked potato salad, so I decided this would be the menu. For me, making the potato salad would be the greater challenge since I didn't like to eat it and actually had never even tasted it. I had seen my mom make potato salad many times, though, so I thought I could probably handle it. First, I peeled and started boiling the potatoes. While the potatoes were boiling I also put two eggs on to boil and began to assemble my other ingredients. I was able to locate a recipe for potato salad in one of my mom's old cookbooks. However, this recipe would feed eight.

With only my mom and possibly my brother Mitch eating it, I figured we certainly wouldn't need enough for eight. Using my best judgment, I decided to half the recipe.

While the potatoes and eggs were boiling, I lifted the pizza kit box from the shelf and began reading the instructions. This was the year 1970, long before the days of pizza delivery. The pizza craze was the Chef-Boy-Are-D in a box, complete with dough mix, sauce, and Parmesan cheese. First, I mixed the crust mix with warm water, placed it in a bowl, and covered it with a clean kitchen dishtowel. The instructions said to place the bowl in a warm place for fifteen minutes. Well, the only warm place I could think of was our oven, and it would only be warm if I turned it on. So, I turned the oven on to about 250 degrees and placed the plastic Tupperware bowl with the dough in it on the top shelf.

By this time, my potatoes and eggs were finished boiling, and I proceeded to put together potato salad for the very first time in my life. I drained the water off of the potatoes and placed them in a bowl. Next, I chopped up the eggs and added them along with mayonnaise, mustard, and sweet pickles. The recipe said to use a dash of salt and pepper, so I quickly sprinkled a little of each on top. With a stir of the spoon, presto, I had created potato salad. I covered my creation with plastic wrap and placed the bowl in the refrigerator to get cold. Now I was ready to finish my pizza.

Carefully, I opened the oven door to see how the pizza dough was rising. Was I ever in for a shock! The pizza dough had risen, but something I hadn't planned for had also happened. The green, plastic bowl had melted itself right into one side of the dough. I was horrified. What on earth could I do now? I quickly grabbed a towel and pulled the bowl, or should I say what was left of it, out of the oven. I had to try to salvage some of the dough if possible, or else my mom would be having potato salad as the main course and only item for her meal.

Mitch, who had absolutely no appreciation for my efforts, decided to walk in the front door at that very moment. I probably could have handled a small chuckle, but rolling in the floor laughing was taking it a bit too far. I ordered him out of the kitchen, and with one last look at the mess I'd made, he took his smiling face back outside with his buddies. With time running out before Mom would be home, I had to try to salvage some of the pizza dough. Once I started digging the dough that wasn't melted out and into another bowl, I realized I had nearly half left. Setting the melted bowl aside for a memory, I then pressed on with rolling out the remainder of the dough. The dough only covered about three fourths of the pizza pan, but I decided that was okay. Next, I added the sauce and sprinkled on the cheese. Once the pizza was ready to go into the oven, I realized I should have only used half of the ingredients for the top since I only had half of the dough left. Oh well, it was too late now. I placed my creation in the oven to bake.

My afternoon had flown by, and my mom would be home soon. I quickly cleaned up the huge mess I had managed to make in the kitchen. Next, I began setting the table for this very special dinner for my mom. In one of our kitchen cabinets I found a candle and candle holder. This would be a nice finishing touch. With the plates, silverware, and glasses all set, and the candle arranged in the center of the table, everything was perfect. I heard the timer go off on our oven and knew the pizza was ready. It actually looked pretty good, considering. I pulled the potato salad from the refrigerator and found just the right spot on the table for it to go. Being extra careful, I struck a match and lit the candle I had found. As soon as I blew out the match, I heard a car door slam. As I peeked out the window, I saw my mom heading toward the front door. She looked tired and her shoulders slumped slightly as she stepped up the cinderblocks to the front door. There I stood as she opened the door with a huge grin on my face. Although I could see the tiredness in her eyes, she smiled as she looked up at me and said, "What are you up to, Jamie?"

"Come on in and see," I encouraged.

As she stepped up the final step and walked in our mobile home door, her eyes traveled instantly to the lit candle on the table. Her small smile enlarged into an enormous one as I proclaimed, "I made your dinner."

With tears in her eyes, she reached for me and hugged me so very tight. I felt proud inside because I had made her day special. As we both sat down to eat, I went on to tell her about the pizza dough episode. If the pizza didn't taste right, she didn't complain. She went on and on about how good the potato salad was and she even had two helpings!

We remembered that night for a long time. I learned that you shouldn't put a plastic bowl in a warm oven, but I also learned how wonderful it is to show someone how much you love them.

GOODNIGHT!

ROAD TRIP

When I was nine years old, my mom, her sister Shirley, and her good friend Jackie Hogston decided to take a trip to Chicago for a convention. Along on that trip were my Aunt Shirley's daughter, Annette, Jackie's three children, Rita, Jerry, and Lisa, and my brother Mitch and me. We didn't go on too many trips so we hadn't bought any luggage. However, my Grandma Justice had a suitcase she let us borrow. We packed it full and loaded it along with the others on top of our 1964 Chevrolet station wagon.

All three women sat up front and all six of us kids piled in the back. Mitch and Jerry took the middle seat behind the women, and all four of us girls were compacted in the way back. We were, of course, arguing and fighting from the very start, being normal kids.

At first, my mom, who was driving, would threaten Mitch and me that she was going to pull over. After awhile, we realized she wasn't and continued our banter. Next, Mitch and Jerry, the only boys, would gang up on us girls, and Jackie would fuss at her son, Jerry. This continued off and on for sometime until finally the women just buried themselves in their own conversation and ignored us. Basically, they left us to duke it out on our own. We had been tuned out. Actually, it worked temporarily because with no one to notice our arguing, we gave it up and decided to get along.

Everyone settled in for a nice, long ride. However, the noise level was still pretty high. Annette and I had convinced Lisa and Rita to join us as we sang every song we ever knew. Of course, the boys couldn't just sit back and enjoy our little concert. They had to join in and sing the wrong words on purpose. This really made our songs sound horrible, but we decided to sing on louder and louder.

It was at that high-note of a moment that I heard the thump. I immediately turned around behind us to see a suitcase bouncing down the highway. The fact that it had flown off of our car was obvious to me, but not so to the women in the front seat.

"Mom," I screamed out. There wasn't a response since the front seat had decided to tune us all out.

"Mom," I shouted louder and began to tell her that our suitcase had fallen off the top of the car.

"Don't be silly," she said as she kept right on with her conversation with Shirley and Jackie.

"Mom," I shouted again. "It really did fall off. Please just look on top of the car and see."

"Jamie, I told you, nothing has fallen off the car!"

"But Mom, I saw it! I think it was Grandma's suitcase."

This at last got her attention. She then decided to pull over and check on top of the car. As she, Aunt Shirley and Jackie got out of the car, we could tell by the looks on their faces that indeed the suitcase was gone.

When they got back in the car, I tried to explain about how far back I thought it was. We had to wait until the next exit to get off and then head back. For once, our station wagon was quiet. I wasn't sure then if we were concerned about what was in the suitcase or the fact that it was one of Grandma Justice's best and maybe only piece of luggage. I noticed Mom driving slower than before, and then we noticed a couple of cars up ahead pulled over to the side of the road.

We drove a little further and then pulled over ourselves. Grandma's suitcase had fallen off the top of our station wagon and bounced across the highway to the other side. A man who was driving right behind this tractor-trailer saw the entire thing, and he proceeded to tell the whole story.

The suitcase flew right off the top, bounced about four times and landed very briefly in the opposite lanes. Without any time lapse, a tractor-trailer, which was moving on down the highway, ran right over the top of it, busting it into several pieces. The contents went flying all up and down the breezy highway.

My mom, Aunt Shirley, and Jackie all were out in the middle of the four-lane highway picking up the remains of what was in the suitcase. All of us kids just sat in the car and watched. We knew better than to even attempt to ask questions or get out of the car at this time. We were pretty solemn at first, but as more and more vehicles stopped to see what was the matter, we couldn't help but laugh. For there were Mom, Aunt Shirley, and Jackie, out there picking up bras, panties, and nightwear that had blown all over the highway. The people along the roadside, being mostly men, were grinning ear to ear and on the verge of bursting out laughing. I guess it was at this point that the women decided to break the ice.

Shirley picked up some undergarments and said, “Are these yours, Nelsene?” talking to my mom. This made the three women laugh, and the bystanders were able to laugh as well. Three women picking up all types of underclothes while the breezy wind blew them everywhere was certainly a sight to see.

Most of our clothes were recovered, and we kept pieces of the suitcase so we could match it up and buy Grandma another one. We had a good trip and a lot of laughs.

I still remember the day we arrived home. Grandma Justice came out to meet us and give everyone a hug. The new suitcase we had bought was tied securely on top of the car. All eyes were watching her as she looked at the piece of luggage. We were all waiting to see if she would notice that it was different.

She looked at Mom and said, “Is this here my piece of luggage, Nelsene?” We all burst out laughing. Grandma looked puzzled.

“I’ll tell you about it later,” my mom said.

GOODNIGHT!

Mitch, Jamie, Scottie, Annette, and Robin in Grandma's front yard in front of the creek.

THE BIG ONE

My Grandma and Grandpa Davis lived in Buchanan County. Their house was right off the highway and their actual address was Raven, Virginia. To get to their house we had to travel over a bridge because there was a creek found directly in front of their house. Most of the time, the creek was about ankle high, but sometimes certain areas were nearly knee deep. If we were going to be playing in the creek, we had to wear shoes because rocks of all shapes, sizes and sharp edges were everywhere. Some days it appeared there were more rocks than water.

When we went to visit Grandma, we would go inside and give her and Grandpa a big hug. Usually, we would eat, basically because that was what you did at your grandparents' house. Next, we children would sit around the living room listening to our parents and grandparents talk about anything and everything. Who was in the hospital and who had recently died usually came up, and we children were bored to tears. Finally, after we felt like we had suffered enough, one of us would get up the nerve to ask if we could go outside.

It's funny how we would always get the same response, "Well, if you kids are finished visiting with us, I guess you can go on outside."

I didn't quite understand why they said that because everyone had been talking ninety miles an hour to each other. Hardly anyone had said a single word to any of us kids. Anyway, we were ready for our escape and usually headed right for the creek.

My brother, Mitch, and I lived in a trailer park, so getting to play in the creek was a real treat for us. Our cousins, Robin and Scottie, who lived next door to Grandma and Grandpa, weren't as thrilled since they could play in the creek anytime. However, they appeased us by going down to the creek and playing with us anyway.

We slowly made our way down the muddy bank, careful not to fall on any jagged rocks. Once we were down the bank, we were smack dab in the middle of the creek. The banks were about ten feet tall on each side. The creek area where we played was always shady and the water always cold. We were immediately on the lookout for minnows and crawdaddies. Scottie, the youngest of us four, saw the first crawdads. I like them well enough, but preferred not to have him show it to me an inch from my eyeballs. Everyone was on the lookout now.

Mitch scooped up some minnows in an old rusty can he had found. I tried to steal-well, borrow his can, but no such luck. I decided to go upstream a little under the bridge and look for my own cup or can. My cousin, Robin, went with me. I could tell already that it was going to be one of those girls with girls and boys with boys days. Robin spotted a cup in the bank area, but when she picked it up, we saw it had several holes in it. That would never do, so we searched on.

Our Great Uncle John lived just a little ways up from the bridge. We were almost at his house when I spotted it. The biggest fish I had ever seen anywhere near this creek went swimming by. I believe it was a trout, and in all of my eight years of playing in the creek, I hadn't ever seen anything bigger than a minnow. I gasped, and Robin assumed I had seen a snake.

"What is it?" she exclaimed.

"It's a fish, a real big, live fish!" I shouted back. He was now swimming his way past me and heading towards Robin.

I thought quick and yelled at the boys, "There's a big fish coming your way, so try to trap him."

"Yeah, right!" Mitch yelled back.

When I started running and slipping on rocks as I ran, I finally got the boys' attention.

"I think she's serious," Mitch told Scottie.

"There, look!" Scottie yelled, and both boys finally spotted the trout.

Quickly, Mitch and Scottie were gathering some large rocks to try to block off the fish before he got past them. Robin and I arrived just as the fish appeared, and we had him trapped. Scottie was so cute when he spoke, "It's a big one. We've caught ourselves a big fish."

Instantly, we knew we had a fun afternoon in store. Imagine a fish aquarium with a fourteen-inch long fish inside.

The area we blocked off was perfect for our catch because the water was almost knee deep. I'm not sure our captive would have survived very long in the ankle deep water. The excitement of watching him swim around and around and then attempt to go back upstream was really cool. We decided to dam up an upstream area around him to give him a pond-like area to swim in. He was so much fun to watch. One minute he would be perfectly still, and the next minute our fish was swimming with pride. A few times he flopped in the water and splashed us all in the face. We had truly made a new friend.

After an hour or so of watching him, Robin and I decided he must be hungry so we went up to the house to get him some bread. We found a plate of leftover cornbread and confiscated most of it. We would throw a small piece on the top of the water and wait very quietly. We'd all jerk when all of a sudden he would jump up and grab it. In a flash, the fish would gobble up every bite.

I should have known that Mitch would eventually try to pick him up, and he did. Our prize fish just jumped right out of Mitch's hands and almost escaped the barricade we had set up. We enjoyed our friend for the rest of the afternoon, and before we knew it our mom and dad were ready to leave and go home.

All four of us agreed to set him free. Slowly, we moved the rocks where our barricade had been, and he was gone in a flash. All of us were thankful for the time we had to enjoy our captive that afternoon, but it was also a pleasure to give him back his freedom. We would all remember the day we caught the big one for a long time to come.

GOODNIGHT!

FIRECRACKER POWDER

To this very day, I don't know why I let my brother talk me into doing the dumbest things. I was, however, responsible for making my own choices, whether right or wrong.

The month was January, and the weather in our Virginia town was brisk and cold. Our Christmas break from school was over, and we were just getting back into our school routine. The streets were all clear from the last snowstorm when a new storm hit. As we sat in our classes at school that day, we watched the snow begin to fall slowly. What began as a trickling snow quickly turned into a blizzard. We actually thought they would send us home early from school, but ended up staying until the 3:15 bell after all. As I rode the school bus home that day, I knew we were in for another break from school.

My brother, Mitch, and I were both excited about staying up late and sleeping in again. The first two days we were outside playing in the snow on and off most of the day. By Thursday that week, it appeared we were going to be home from school for the rest of the week. Normally we would have loved all of this time off, but we had just recently finished up our Christmas break. So, actually we were kind of looking forward to seeing and playing with our friends again from school.

Boredom began to creep in by Thursday afternoon, and that was about the time trouble found us, or maybe it was us who found trouble. At any rate, we were about to embark on a new invention.

I could try to blame my dad for how that January day ended, but really he had taught us better. My dad was a kid at heart and always loved fireworks. I actually remember us setting off more fireworks in the winter than summer. Christmas was a big opportunity to set off fireworks for my dad. He must have saved some for later because Mitch managed to find them. Next came one of Mitch's brainstorm ideas.

"Let's take the firecrackers and break them in half, and then empty the powder in a little bowl," he suggested.

"What for?" I asked.

"So we can set it on fire," was his reply.

"No way," I said. "Mom told us never to play with matches, especially in the house."

"Okay then, we'll light the match outside," was his comeback.

"You know what I meant," I said smartly.

"Oh, come on," he pleaded, "we will only light a few."

I was going soft, and with his suave, convincing voice, I finally agreed to go along with him.

"The powder is probably not any good anymore anyway," Mitch went on to say.

"Okay," I said. "What do we need to do?"

Mitch had me go and find a small container to pour the powder in. I looked everywhere trying to find something sturdy enough that wouldn't catch on fire. As I was about to give up, I found the perfect thing under the kitchen sink. It was a small glass ashtray that my mom kept around for when people who smoked visited us. I ran to where Mitch was and showed him the ashtray.

"Perfect," he said.

While I had been on my search, Mitch had found a few more firecrackers hidden in a junk drawer in the living room. When I looked at the heap on the floor, I realized what started as a few firecrackers was now a mountain of them. I sat down beside Mitch and began to take the firecrackers one by one and break them in half. We would then sprinkle the powder into our ashtray. Only small amounts came out of each one.

We soon realized that it was going to take all afternoon to completely fill the ashtray at this rate of speed. We decided a half-inch deep would certainly be enough for our little experiment, and accomplishing this would only take a little longer.

After about fifty or more were emptied of their powder, we decided we had enough. Grabbing our coats, we gently picked up our ashtray of firecracker powder and headed outside. Mitch, of course, was doing the honors of lighting the match. I was the one who had to hold the powder filled ashtray. There's an interesting thing about ashtrays. Ashtrays have a groove for the cigarette they are holding. My little thumb fit perfectly in that groove, and this is how I was holding it when Mitch struck the match.

I'm not sure what either of us expected, but the enormous flame that burst up was not it. The whole ashtray basically caught on fire for a matter of seconds, and seconds was all it took for my injury to occur.

Without thinking I dropped the glass ashtray on the sidewalk, and began screaming hysterically. The ashtray broke in pieces on the cement, but I had pains of my own. That right thumb that had fit so nicely in the groove of the ashtray was beet red and hurting really bad.

"Are you okay, sis?" My brother quickly asked.

"No, I'm not," I said through tears. "My thumb feels like it's on fire."

"Let's go inside and put in under cold water," he said.

With tears rolling down my cheeks, I turned to follow him inside. We ran cold water over the burn for several minutes, but this wasn't easing the pain. I knew Mitch was scared for me when he announced he was going next door to get our grandma.

In a matter of minutes, Grandma came walking in, and as she noticed the pile of broken firecrackers on the floor, she exclaimed, "What have you two done now?"

I showed her my thumb, and she took me to her house and put some first aid spray on it. This helped some, but I could still see the ashtray going up in flames in my mind. The rest of the day was spent listening to our grandma continually telling us what and all could have happened worse.

"You kids could have set the trailer on fire or burned your eyes out," she said. Grandma's list just went on and on like that all afternoon.

Down deep we knew she was right, but it had seemed like a good idea at the time. Within a few days the pain subsided, but my thumbnail turned coal black. A week following, I realized my nail was ruined.

As I sat in my third grade class one day picking at my nail, the whole thumbnail peeled completely off. This was a gruesome sight and very painful as well. I thought of my brother at that moment and wondered how I let him convince me to take firecracker powder and set it on fire.

Needless to say, neither of us ever did that little trick again.

GOODNIGHT!

SNAKE ON THE PATH

When I was young, most of my friends lived in mobile homes like me. At age eight, our family moved our mobile home to a different mobile home park in a place called Hill Creek. The name Hill Creek wasn't a very exciting name, but neither was the place most days.

About a mile from my home was a winding dirt road that led to my friend Tammy's house. One boring summer day, two of my friends from the mobile home park, Angela and Pat, and I decided to walk to Tammy's house to play. They referred to the area Tammy lived in as the "holler." A holler to us was a place where only four-wheel drive vehicles could venture. Several kids I knew at school lived in hollers and could not drive their family car all the way to their house. The roads were narrow and bumpy and most cars would end up dragging bottom the whole way. Shade trees lined both sides of the path that led to Tammy's house, so the walk was going to be a relief from the heat on this hot summer day.

The Hogston kids lived on our way, so we stopped to see if they wanted to join us. Rita wasn't as excited about coming as Jerry and Lisa were, but she joined us anyway. Our journey up the winding dirt path included skipping, walking, and cutting up all the way. Being out of the baking sun and among the shady trees made for a pleasant break. The long walk had to be annoying to Tammy when she made it all the time just to catch the school bus or to go anywhere. For us, though, it was a fun adventure.

We skipped along noisily, the thought of danger never entering our minds. Looking back now, I forget who saw him first, but the shock on everyone's face showed instantly. Right in the middle of the path we were treading was a big, fat, vicious rattlesnake. He was everything we had ever imagined in a snake and more. This critter had those beady eyes and a long, quick, slithery tongue. He was huge and had wrapped himself up in a coil-like position. The rattler on the end of his tail was making a subtle, creepy sound that captivated all of our attention. Minutes must have ticked by before any of us spoke a word or moved a muscle.

Jerry was the first to speak, "We've got to kill him." This statement shocked us all into reality.

Rita, the oldest, took the first plan of action. She started looking around and with a confident voice said, "We'll need some big rocks."

The thought of turning back and heading home never crossed any of our minds. We were on our way to our friend's house, and this snake was only an obstacle that we would need to conquer along the way.

We decided as a group to move in very slow movements and search for the biggest rocks we could possibly find. Jerry, being the only boy along and the daring type, decided he would throw the first rock. I believe somehow in his tiny brain he had convinced himself that one hearty blow from him would defeat our enemy. We all backed up and with watchful eyes gazed upon the target as Jerry threw the huge, jagged rock right at the snake.

Crunch! The rock landed in a slam on the back of the snake's body. Instantly, the snake's body jerked, leaving us all screaming. He began to slither and rattle with more vigor than before. Everyone was a good distance away, but I still felt like at any minute he could have us on the run. The rock Jerry threw wounded the snake, but he was far from being harmless.

Rita, Jerry's older sister, was ready to take her turn next. "Look out!" She shouted and everyone backed up a little further. The rock she threw missed the snake by several feet and had our angry friend slithering even more.

I was ready to take my turn. Even with my racing heart, I felt I could land a good blow and maybe even defeat this enemy. I must have envisioned the bigger the better when I chose my rock, because the one I chose was entirely too heavy for me. This became evident to everyone when it landed not three feet in front of the snake, but three feet in front of me. They needed an icebreaker to relieve tension, and my blunder was it. Everyone burst out laughing. The laughter was short lived as the snake began slithering toward Lisa.

Lisa, who was only five and the baby of the group, didn't warn any of us of her intent. She had a decent size rock aimed at the snake and surprisingly enough hit him right in the neck. Lisa was quite proud of herself, until we all realized that this second injury had only made our slithering friend all the angrier.

With two injuries causing obvious pain, the snake began moving in Jerry's direction. We all gasped in horror as Jerry took the rocks in his hands and again hit our enemy. The snake slowly moved the other direction, but still lay undefeated.

For about the next hour we each took turns throwing rocks at this very courageous snake who seemed more like a cat with nine lives. Many of our throws were complete misses, landing nowhere near him. With each throw the snake would eye his attacker, slither his tongue, and rattle his tail. The whole event was eerie. No one knew who threw the final blow or if it were a series of hits, but finally the snake fell over defeated.

As we looked at him in his crumpled state, he didn't have the same hold on us as he had before. He lay there in a mountain of rocks of all sizes, some that had caused injury and many that didn't even come close.

Exhausted from the whole ordeal, we looked at each other and felt the victory surge among us. With a sense of accomplishment and pride we each strutted past our enemy with our heads held high. More than ready to continue our journey to Tammy's house, we pressed on.

Our pace picked up measurably as we neared her house, each of us anxious to share our victory with our friend. Tammy heard us approach and came out to greet us. We all interrupted each another as we attempted to tell her our snake crisis. When we quieted for a moment to hear her response, she confidently put her hands on her hips and said, "I don't believe a word of it!"

Stunned by her statement, we quickly grabbed her arm and said, "Come on, we'll show you."

"This isn't necessary," she shouted as we dragged her along, but we just kept going.

As we neared our opponent, we all slowed our pace, just being cautious of course. When Tammy was close enough to see, she gasped and said, "Well, I would never have believed it!"

Jerry chose that moment to sneak up behind us all and make a distinct hissing sound. We all jumped as though the snake were coming back to life. Jerry's goofy joke had us all smiling and laughing too. After what we had experienced, we were ready for a good laugh. We left our foe there in the middle of the road, and headed back to Tammy's house. The rest of the day was spent telling anyone who would listen of our great victory, and the story growing in detail each time it was told.

GOODNIGHT!

Mitch crashing the P.J. party

THE PAJAMA PARTY

You only turn nine years old once, and I had made it my personal mission to have a special party. I started early on buttering up my mom for an all night sleepover, or shall I say pajama party. My mom worked long hours, and I knew planning a party and giving up her much needed sleep was a real sacrifice. My birthday was April the 29, so I wasn't taking any chances. I decided to start my personal mission right after Christmas.

The middle of January was upon us, and I thought this was a perfect time to put a little bug in her ear. I just let her know that my birthday was only three short months away. I went ahead and dove right in with my idea to have a pajama party. Her response was, "We'll see."

I knew that would have to suffice for now. At least she didn't say no. I let the subject rest with her, but my mind was going ninety miles per hour making mental plans. My intention was to bring up the subject once or twice a month until April. However, my forgetfulness in February put a damper on that idea. My fourth grade teacher was planning a school Valentine Party for February 14, and I raised my hand and volunteered to bring cupcakes. There was only one problem with this cupcake thing. I forgot to tell my mom about it until about 7:00 pm on February 13. She hurriedly ran out and was up late making cupcakes that night. I decided after my little slip-up about the cupcakes, I would have to pass on mentioning the pajama party in February.

The March winds blew in our Virginia town with a vengeance. One March evening while we were stuck inside, I got brave and decided to mention the pajama party again. My answer this time was worth waiting for. "I don't see why not," my mom said. For me, that was a big yes.

For the next nine weeks, my mind and mouth went one hundred miles per hour. My mom probably wished she had waited until the day before the party to give me my answer. Where would we sleep? What would we eat? What games would we play? The list of questions went on and on.

We lived in a very small two-bedroom mobile home, so space was limited. We would have to sleep in-between the living area, which was located in between Mom's bedroom and the kitchen. I was given a limit on how many I could invite, so I had to narrow my list way down. I finally had the perfect list. I would be inviting Rita, Lisa, my cousin Annette, and several friends from school. The date was set and plans were being made. I knew we would have cake, ice cream, and popcorn for a late night snack. What I hadn't planned on was the cool games my mom would come up with for us to play.

With the big night only a few days away, my mom was ready to make a trip to the grocery store. She let me choose the flavor of cake to make, and I chose chocolate with chocolate frosting. We decided together on Neapolitan ice-cream, so everyone could choose chocolate, vanilla, or strawberry. We picked up a package of candles, and I was already so excited that I wasn't sure I could even sleep a single night until the party.

The big night finally arrived, and I waited impatiently for my guests to arrive. We had cleaned house, Mom had made and frosted the cake, and already I had two presents sitting on the table by the cake. Just when I thought I couldn't wait another second, there was a knock at the door and my first guests, Lisa and Rita, had arrived. They were sisters, and although Lisa was younger than me, I invited her anyway so she wouldn't feel left out. The rest of the girls arrived nearly all at one time, and we all plopped down in the living room area to visit. We talked, and giggled for about the first hour. Next, my mom suggested that I open my gifts. I remember getting two Barbie dolls, some jewelry, and a purse. All the gifts were great, and I was floating on a cloud. My mom had everyone sing Happy Birthday to me, and then we dove into the cake and ice cream. I was certainly glad we had chosen Neapolitan because it seemed everyone liked a different flavor. Time had really flown by, and we all agreed it was time to go and get our pajamas on.

Once in our pajamas, we gathered in a circle and played about six rounds of truth or dare. The last dare was for Lisa to press her lips up to the living room mirror and stay in that position. Just then, Mom entered the room and announced she had a game planned, rescuing Lisa. She had each of us put a blindfold around our eyes while we remained sitting in the circle. Next she dumped a huge pile of panty hose in the floor in the middle of us.

"You girls are having a pantyhose race," she announced. "The girl wearing the most pair of hose in the end is the winner," she went on to say.

When Mom told us to start, we were to begin putting on panty hose as fast as we could. What we weren't told was that with all the hose thrown together in a pile, we could only get one leg in and someone else could have the other leg. Before we could think it through, my mom blurted out "Go!" and we were off.

We pulled and strained and laughed and giggled while we tried desperately to put on the hose. My mom must have enjoyed watching because she, too, was laughing hysterically. We continued until there weren't any hose left in the pile to pick up.

"You can take off your blindfolds now!" my mom declared.

As we removed the blindfolds, our laughter intensified. We were certainly a funny looking bunch. I had about six pair of hose on, except that with four of those pairs, I only had one leg, and my friends had their legs in the other half. We all looked hilariously ridiculous. We managed to get out of the hose at about the same speed we had put them on. We were huddled in our little group when my mom told us to just talk and have fun for now and that she would pop popcorn later. She then ventured off to her bedroom for some peace and quiet.

Well, we talked and laughed and giggled and had great fun. Every girl seemed to have something exciting to share with each other. We talked of school, boys, friends and every other topic under the sun. Life was grand, or at least we thought it was until, without warning, my brother Mitch appeared. He was supposed to be staying the night with friends, but just popped in for a little visit. We girls had already unfolded our sleeper couch into a bed and were all sitting in a circle.

Mitch jumped right in the middle of us as he shouted, “Hello girls, room for one more at your party?”

Naturally we all screamed, as we shouted, “No!”

His little plan to spoil the party was quickly put to an end when Mom came walking in.

“Out, Mitch!” she exclaimed. Mitch grinned his goofy grin and off he went back to his friend’s house.

My mom gave us all a big smile and asked if we were ready for popcorn. We were and waited patiently while smelling the buttery scent of popcorn in the air. Two huge bowls filled to the top were delivered to our circle on the sofa. We decided to skip watching television and just talk. So, we ate and talked and talked and ate. The walls were pretty thin in our small mobile home, so at midnight Mom turned out the lights and we knew that meant bedtime. We still talked quietly, but before long we had all dozed off.

The next thing I remember was the smell of pancakes and syrup. My mom was the best. Everyone started talking all at once as they woke up, and we all veered to the kitchen table. The pancakes were delicious. Breakfast was over and all too soon Moms were picking up their daughters to go home. The last guest to leave was my cousin Annette. As she and my Aunt Shirley pulled out of the driveway, I looked over at my mom and smiled. I ran over into Mom's arms and gave her the biggest, longest hug as I thanked her for the best P.J. party ever.

GOODNIGHT!

CEMETERY HILL

Living less than a mile from the town's scariest cemetery certainly had its advantages and disadvantages. The neatest thing about this cemetery was the rolling hills. The kids in my trailer park and I loved to ride bikes. Cemetery hill was a bikers' heaven with all those winding hills. An afternoon bike ride usually concluded with a ride through the cemetery. Once in a while, we would ride over by the cemetery when the sun was going down, but we were never there after dark.

This particular summer day started off like many others. My friends and I began our day playing around the trailer park and eventually decided to ride bikes. We rode around the winding road just beyond our mobile home. Next, we took turns doing stunts on a makeshift ramp we had found. As always, a day of bike riding wasn't complete until we rode up and down cemetery hill.

Even in the daylight I would get a creepy feeling riding around near all those gravesites. The outside entrance resembled something from an old horror movie. Two gothic iron gates were at the opening, and at night they were closed and locked tight. My worst nightmare would be getting stuck on the wrong side of those iron gates after dark.

Anyway, my friends and I pedaled with all our might to make it up the first couple of hills. Once you made it up the first one, if you kept up your speed, then you could coast up and down the next. We had a great time just riding around. One of my friends named Charlie could glide down some of the hills without having his hands on the handlebars. I would try that on straight roads, but not on a hill. At last we topped over the last hill and eased right back out of the entrance gate.

Right in front of the entrance was a plush, grassy area, and we all decided to sit down for a breather. While sitting on the grass in the cool shade, we all started making up our own stories about things that were supposed to have happened at night in the cemetery. Everyone's story seemed a little more unbelievable as they told it. My turn came, and I just said that I wasn't afraid of anything in that old cemetery. I went on to say that everyone there was already dead anyway.

"Well," Ronald said, "If you're not afraid, Jamie, then I dare you to ride your bike through the cemetery tonight."

Ronald had certainly called my bluff, and I don't think he wanted to be outdone by a girl. Looking back now, I should have just made up an excuse or something, but my big mouth got the best of me.

"I'm not afraid, if that's what you mean," I answered right to his face.

"Well then?" Ronald replied.

"I'll do it!" I blurted before I even knew I had opened my mouth.

All of my friends looked at me as if I had lost my mind. I believe I did for a few split seconds, but the dare was on. We all grabbed our bikes and headed home for supper, knowing it would be dark soon enough.

I could normally eat two plates of spaghetti, but not tonight. Half of my first plate was still there when I exited the table. Darkness came early that night, and when I looked outside the trailer window, there they were with their bikes waiting. My so-called friends were going to escort me to the entrance, and supposedly they were going to wait for me there.

I couldn't put it off any longer. Out the front door I went, not saying a word to my awaiting audience. I picked up my bike, and we were off in a flash. My heart was racing wildly as we rode our bikes toward the cemetery. We made it to the front entrance in record time, and I knew my moment had come. For once, I wished I had just kept my big mouth shut. Everyone stopped with me at the entrance, and I knew I needed to start pedaling or start confessing that I was afraid like everyone else. I chose that moment to start pedaling, and I didn't dare look back.

Fortunately, I had a headlight on my bicycle, so I could see even though it was getting darker by the minute. I rode over the first hill, trying desperately not to look to my left or my right at the tombstones beside the graves. If I could just pretend I was somewhere else and keep pedaling, I was sure I could make it. As I pedaled faster, my heart raced faster and I decided to concentrate only on getting over the next hill. With my hands clenched tightly on the handlebars, I strolled up and down each hill. There was only one hill left in the distance, and then I could just circle the curve and be on my way back. However, as I topped over this last hill, a shadow by the gravesite straight ahead got my attention, and as I looked away I lost my balance. I was able, just before I crashed, to steer toward the grassy area. This move enabled me to land on grass and not crash on the pavement. My headlight started flickering from the crash, and as I got up off the grass I noticed to my right a tombstone. When I started to back away from the tombstone, I felt an unexpected dip behind me. Almost too afraid to look, I realized what the dip was. I was standing right in the center of a sunken grave. Naturally, I started imagining movement and noises and all kinds of strange things.

For an instant I was frozen and couldn't move, but suddenly I remembered the front gate would be closed and locked soon. I quickly grabbed my bicycle and with all the energy I had left, started pedaling frantically. I knew I had to get out of there quickly. The faster I pedaled, the more I just knew someone was behind me. I never did look back. As I rounded the last curve and topped over the last hill, my headlight began to flicker and dimmed almost completely out. I could see the entrance in sight and just hoped my headlight would make it until I got out of there. The entrance was now in view, and I was almost there. My friends were waiting and I could see two of them in the shadows ahead. Just a few more seconds and I would be home free, but a voice suddenly startled me.

"Get out of here! You want to get locked up in here all night?" A voice yelled.

Out the front entrance I rode, just as the cemetery keeper closed the iron gates and locked them securely. The girls were cheering for me as I crossed the imaginary finish line.

Ronald and Charlie couldn't believe I had done it. They weren't about to congratulate me, so they just grabbed their bikes and explained, "We need to be getting home."

The girls, however, began asking me all sorts of questions.

"Was it scary? Did you see anything strange? Were you afraid?"

Finally able to catch my breath I answered, "Who, me? Scared? Uh, not really!" I said as I grabbed my bike and we headed home.

GOODNIGHT!

MAN OF WAR
(THE JELLYFISH)

My dad loved to fish and we made our way to the ocean more than one summer. I was most likely only five or six years old the first time I saw the ocean. As my bare feet stepped across the sand, the warm grains trickled their way up between my toes. I remember the sand either tickled or burned them the moment I stepped onto the beach. The seashells lying all along the shore always got my immediate attention. I would walk along the shore gathering as many as I could hold. Then I would carry them to my sand bucket where I emptied them handful by handful.

Once I could focus past the gathering of seashells, I would fix my eyes on the ocean. The ocean was bigger than any type of lake or river I had ever seen. The water seemed to go on forever. Within seconds my staring eyes told my warming feet to take off running for the waves ahead.

As I ran through the water, two small waves greeted me and knocked me underwater. I jumped up smiling with the taste of salt water in my mouth. Yes, I knew it. I had arrived at the ocean.

The summer I was twelve years old we were at Myrtle Beach in South Carolina. Dad was not with us this year because he and my mom had divorced several years before. On this trip, I was with my mom and new step-dad, John. Our motel was right by the beach. The weather was perfect, and I knew we had an awesome week in store.

I played that first afternoon constantly in the waves, only coming ashore once to build a sandcastle. My sandcastle adventure lasted well over an hour. I probably would have only built on my castle for a few minutes if I had been alone, but then some other kids joined me. Together we built an enormous sand castle with a moat.

The first day at the beach came to an end, and we showered and left to go out to dinner. We walked through some market places where you could find just about anything to buy. My step-dad, John, wanted seafood so we ended up at a fancy seafood restaurant. I didn't mind because they had hamburgers and French fries on the menu. After we ate we made our way back to the motel for the evening.

I was glad to get back to our room. My day on the beach had exhausted me, and I was ready for the bed. I lay down and was fast asleep the moment my head hit the pillow.

I knew I had slept soundly when the sun's glimmer came through the window the next morning, fully covering my pillow. As I rolled over, stretching and yawning, I knew another great day at the beach was awaiting me. My mom and step-dad were having a late breakfast later, so I fixed myself some cereal and enjoyed a cartoon while I ate. As soon as I was finished eating, I quickly dressed into my bathing suit, grabbed a towel and headed toward the beach. I had made friends with some other kids the day before, and they were there waiting for me.

The ocean water was cold, so we opted to begin building a sand castle. This didn't last long, because watching everyone in the water compelled us up and into the water ourselves. We had only been in the water a few minutes when my mom and step-dad made their way to the beach. I waved and tried to coax Mom into the water. She shook her head no as she yelled, "Maybe later when it's warmer."

I went back to playing with my new friends. The ocean water was murky that hot afternoon, and we were unable to see the bottom. Occasionally, twigs or seaweed would float by and tickle my legs. Once or twice I even had to untangle a piece that made its way around my foot.

We were in water up to our chests catching waves and throwing a beach ball around when I was distracted by another piece of seaweed. This piece of seaweed, or at least what I thought was seaweed, wrapped around my leg just below the knee. Only this time, the seaweed came with an instant stinging feeling. I quickly took my hand down under the murky water to get it off. The seaweed then wrapped itself around my hand, and my hand began stinging too. Becoming frantic, I jerked my hand up out of the water and saw that there was a swollen white whelp all across the top of my hand. Immediately, I started screaming. "Something's got me, I've been bitten!"

My friends weren't sure how to help without harming themselves. I wanted to run, but was afraid to move. I was crying frantically now, as I saw my mom approaching me. My screaming had obviously gotten the attention of a lot of people, mainly the lifeguard. He was headed toward me, right behind my mom. I grabbed my mom's hand as the lifeguard grabbed me and we made our way back to shore.

The lifeguard had me sit down as soon as we were on shore. The white whelp across my hand was swelling rapidly. As he examined my leg, he found an identical whelp there that wrapped itself almost all the way around my leg.

As he placed ice packs on my hand and leg, tears were rolling down my face. Both parts were stinging like a bee sting and felt like they were on fire. The lifeguard then started explaining to my mom what had bitten me. He told her that I had not been the first person bitten this season. Several others had come ashore crying like me. The creature is actually called "Man of War" and is similar to a Jellyfish, the lifeguard explained to us. They float through the water stinging anything in their way. He went on to tell my mom that there was really nothing they could do except place an ice pack over the swollen areas. He also said I would be in a lot of pain and probably would run a fever for two or three days. Some people even have flu like symptoms, the lifeguard said. As my step-dad carried me back to our motel room, I said good-bye to my new friends.

As I lay there in bed that afternoon, I couldn't help but keep looking at the whelps. Every time I did, the pain seemed to worsen. I think part of it was because I would imagine this scary creature swimming through the ocean and attacking me again. My mom gave me Tylenol, and I finally rested that afternoon. I woke up around suppertime in pain again.

The pain did lighten up after the first day. However, the swelling didn't go down until later. I watched all the cartoons anyone could possibly imagine lying there in the motel room bed. My mom and step-dad did feel sorry for me and spoil me those two and a half days in bed. They would bring me anything and everything I asked for, within reason of course.

Altogether, I remained in bed nearly three whole days. The swelling finally went down and the stinging stopped, but I had scars for quite a while afterwards. We agreed on the third day that I could go back down to the beach. I was excited and scared, too. I dressed in my swimsuit and made my way through the sand with my mom. When I looked out over the ocean, the fun and excitement wasn't quite there. Some of the friends I had made earlier called from the water, "Come on out, the water's fine."

"Maybe later," I yelled back.

I just couldn't do it that day. I grabbed the sand bucket and started collecting some seashells. My friends did come out of the water long enough to see my scars from the whelps, but then they were back catching waves.

I sat down and began working on a sand castle. I hadn't been working on my castle too long when two of the kids joined me. We had a great time. Our vacation at the beach lasted two more days. I never did go back in the ocean that summer…for obvious reasons. In fact, it was two years later when I finally got up the courage to go back in. Even today, many, many years later, when our family goes to the beach, my first few steps into the water are hard to take.

GOODNIGHT!

ABOUT THE AUTHOR

Jamie Bryant was born in the small town of Richlands, Virginia. Her family moved to Tazewell, Virginia when she was eleven, and she graduated from Tazewell High School. She married Dennis Bryant at age eighteen and they have three children: Jared, Boaz and Cherith. Dennis' enlistment in the USAF took them to Illinois, California, England, and Texas, where they now reside.

Jamie has worked as a home childcare provider for eighteen years, caring for over one hundred children. Currently she is employed as a nanny for three young girls. She has written a series of children's books and several plays. Jamie's writings bring to life the joys and trials of the growing up years with remarkable poignancy.

Printed in the United States
1063900005B/394-495

9 781403 367488